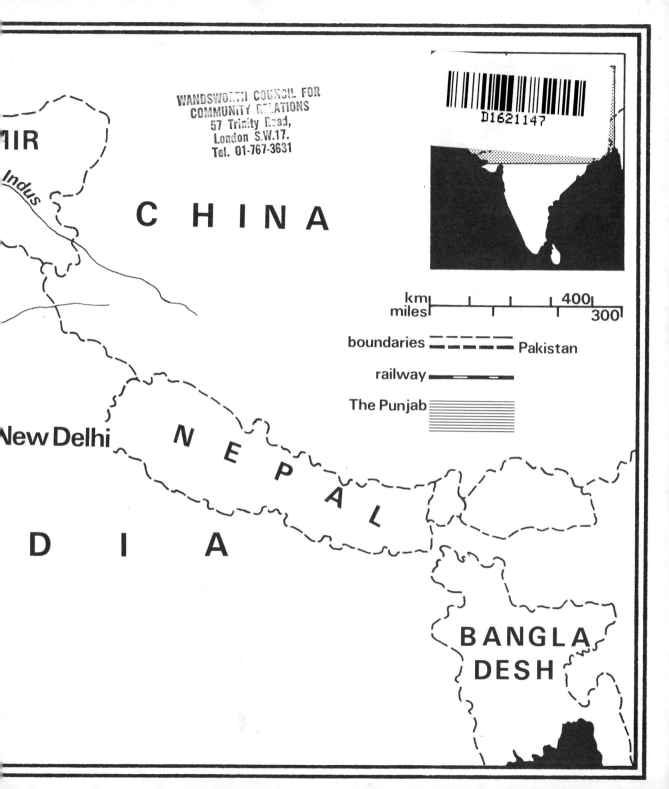

MIR

Indus

C H I N A

D1621147

km
miles

400
300

boundaries   Pakistan

railway

The Punjab

New Delhi

N E P A L

D I A

BANGLA
DESH

Scarsbrook, Ailsa
    Pakistani village. – (Beans).
    I. Title II. Scarsbrook, Alan
    III. Series
    823'. 9'1J   P27.S/
    ISBN 0-7136-1976-7

A & C Black (Publishers) Limited
35 Bedford Row, London WC1R 4JH
ISBN 0 7136 1976 7
Printed in Great Britain by
Hazell, Watson & Viney Ltd, Aylesbury, Bucks.

Pakistani Village

Ailsa and Alan Scarsbrook

Adam & Charles Black · London

This is Assim Mahmood. He lives with his mother and father and two sisters in the village of Dhamial, five kilometres from the big town of Rawalpindi in northern Pakistan.

Assim is fourteen years old. He goes to a boys' school in Rawalpindi, and he gets up early in the morning because he has to cycle a long way to school.

Assim works hard at his lessons because he wants to pass his exams, and then he can go to the military college at Murree and train to be an army officer. Assim's father was once a soldier.

Life is peaceful in Dhamial. The young children play out in the fields during the long sunny days. Their older brothers and sisters go to the boys' school or the girls' school in the village. Assim's younger sister, Teybah, goes to the girls' school.

The women are busy in their homes. Some men, like Mr Sabir, the tailor, travel into Rawalpindi to work.

Other men work in the fields around Dhamial, growing maize and wheat and vegetables, and looking after their goats, oxen and buffalo. Assim's father farms some land in the village.

Most houses in Dhamial are single storey buildings made of bricks, sometimes covered with hard, baked clay. They have flat roofs and wooden window shutters and doors.

The wooden window shutters are closed to keep out the hot sunlight. This makes the rooms inside rather dark, but it helps to keep them nice and cool.

Dhamial has four mosques, a mill, some shops, two schools and a village council meeting house, as well as the houses. There are several wells where the villagers can get water.

Many of the village streets are narrow and winding. This means that the children in Dhamial can play happily without having to bother about any traffic.

Assim lives in one of the bigger houses of the village. On the ground floor there is a courtyard with several rooms leading off – dining room, living room and kitchen.

Upstairs, there are several bedrooms, a bathroom and a balcony. Assim often sleeps out on the balcony or on the flat roof during the hot summer nights.

Assim's mother looks after the house and cooks the meals on a charcoal fire. Shahida, Assim's elder sister, helps her.

All the family like to eat lamb or beef with rice, some potatoes, a good vegetable curry and chapattis. Assim likes to eat plenty of juicy melons and mangoes in the summer time. After a meal, the family drink tea and Assim's father smokes a pipe called a *hookah*.

Assim's mother makes her own clothes on the sewing machine. Pakistani women and girls wear a *dupatta* (scarf), *kamiz* (tunic) and *shalwar* (trousers). Here you can see Assim's mother weaving the *nara* (belt) for her *shalwar*.

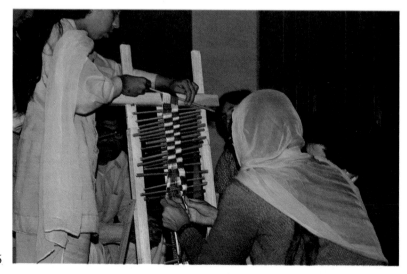

Assim and his family are Muslims – they pray to Allah (God) five times a day and read the Koran. Assim goes with his father to pray at the village mosque. Here is Assim's grandmother saying her prayers, facing towards Mecca.

During the holy month of Ramadan, Assim's parents fast. They do not eat or drink between sunrise and sunset. At the end of Ramadan, the family celebrates the festival of Eid, when they have a feast, put on new clothes and visit friends.

These village women are bringing water home from the well. They balance the heavy jars on a cloth ring which they put on their heads. Water keeps cool in these jars which are made of clay.

The well is worked by oxen, which are blindfolded and walk round in a circle, turning the wooden wheels. The wheels drive a chain of buckets.

The buckets dip into the water deep down in the well, and are then lifted up over the wheel at the top, where the water spills out into a trough. Some villages also have tube wells with electric pumps.

Most of Pakistan has very little rain. The farmers living
on the Punjab plain depend for water upon a huge
system of irrigation canals, leading from the River
Indus and its tributaries. Without water, the
farmers could not grow their crops.

Assim has several friends, who live in another
village, where the villagers grow many different
kinds of vegetables – spinach, onions, cucumbers,
marrows, bhindi and carrots. They water the fields
by irrigation channels leading from two wells.

In Dhamial, most farmers till their land with a wooden plough, pulled by oxen. The farmers would like to use tractors but they are very expensive. Only a few farmers in Dhamial can afford a tractor.

In April or May, the farmers harvest the wheat. They cut it and lay it on an area of flat ground. Then they make yoked oxen walk round in a circle, trampling the wheat until it becomes a heap of crushed straw, husks and grain.

After this, the farmers toss the wheat into the air with their wooden forks. The wind blows the chaff away and lets the heavy grain fall to the ground. The grain is collected and put into sacks.

When he is on holiday from school, Assim sometimes goes along to the mill to watch the miller at work. The miller is proud of the oil engine which turns the big grindstone. It is a new one and was made in Pakistan.

When the engine is working, you can hear its familiar 'poop poop' sound all over the village. This lets the villagers know that the miller is at work and will grind their sacks of corn into flour for them.

Assim likes to go into Rawalpindi with his father to buy things from the market. They often travel by bus, but the buses get very crowded.

The rack on this bus roof is really meant for luggage, but the bus is full up inside, so the men have climbed up on top.

In the towns, the police do not allow passengers to ride on the roof of the bus. Many people also travel in *tongas* (horse-drawn carts).

Rawalpindi is a very busy city and the streets are always crowded. Many shop signs and advertisement boards are written in Urdu and English. Some men dress in western style and some in Pakistani style – with shirt and *shalwar*.

The water seller is kept busy supplying water to the city shop-keepers. His skin bag is a buffalo hide. He fills his bag from a tap on the street.

The shops and stalls in the market sell all kinds of things. This fruit stall has apples, oranges, bananas, guavas and sweet juicy kainos, which look like large tangerines and are only grown in Pakistan.

Assim's father likes to buy fruit for the family and in the hot summer he brings home lovely juicy melons and mangoes.

At another stall, a man cuts long sticks of sugar cane into small pieces which people like to chew for the juice. The large block of ice on top of the pieces of sugar cane is there to keep them cool.

This stall sells salt and spices – chillies and haldi. Pakistanis enjoy spicy foods and meat is often prepared as curry with spices and eaten with rice. Spices are also used when making kebabs, which are rather like beefburgers and are cooked over a charcoal fire.

Assim always makes his father stop at the sweet stall. The sight of all those sweets makes his mouth water.

Sometimes, his mother makes them at home when friends come to visit. She uses butter, sugar, milk, flour and almonds, and decorates them with pista and silver leaf.

Assim likes to watch the craftsmen at work in the market. Some make pottery in various colours and some hammer beautiful patterns on copper bowls and plates, while others make very fine jewellery in gold and silver.

This craftsman is making a *charpoy*, a piece of furniture that serves as a bed in the house and as a couch for resting on out of doors. The charpoy can be made with jute string, or strips of leather or webbing. A gap is left at the top, then laced with strings that can be tightened if the rope sags.

One of the streets near the market is decorated for a wedding. All the relatives and friends of the bride and bridegroom meet together to celebrate this special occasion.

The bride wears a beautifully embroidered red *gharara* and golden shawl. Her necklaces, bracelets, rings and head ornaments are all made of pure gold. She has decorated the palms of her hands with reddish-brown patterns, made by using henna.

The bridegroom wears garlands of money notes given to him by his relatives. Everything that the bride will need in her new home is provided by the bride's family.

19

One day, Assim and his father go to a festival in a nearby village. The festival is a competition between pairs of oxen yoked to the well wheel.

The blindfolded oxen race round and round the well in a circle, and the pair that can race round the greatest number of times in ten minutes are the winners.

While the animals race around fireworks are let off, and musicians play drums, bagpipes and trumpets.

A great crowd of people watches the competition. Seven pairs of oxen take it in turns to race round the well. Assim and his father are very glad that they are standing in the shade of a mango tree, because the midday sun is very hot.

The competition judges announce the winning pair and the crowd cheers. This pair of oxen have raced round the well 145 times in ten minutes. They are decorated and their proud owner receives a prize. Then he rides back home on horseback with his son.

21

In his geography lessons at school, Assim's teacher has told him about the Tarbela Dam on the River Indus, about one hundred kilometres from Rawalpindi.

The dam was completed in 1976, and is the biggest rock and earth filled dam in the world. It will help to produce more electricity for factories, offices, shops and houses. The water it supplies will irrigate the land, and the farmers will be able to grow more crops.

Many people, though, had to leave their homes and go to live in other towns and villages, so that this huge dam could be built.

The Awami express stops at Rawalpindi railway station on its journey from Peshawar (North-West Frontier) via Lahore to Karachi.

During the summer holidays, Assim sometimes travels by train from Rawalpindi to Lyallpur to visit his uncle. He enjoys the journey, and when the train stops at a station he is able to buy all kinds of things to eat and drink.

His uncle works at one of the big mills in Lyallpur. He takes Assim around the mill and shows him the looms weaving beautiful patterns in the cloth.

A lot of cotton is grown in Pakistan. The textile industry is one of the largest industries in the country.

In Assim's favourite section of the mill there are large looms which embroider very intricate patterns on coloured nylon cloth. There are so many different patterns and colours to choose from that Assim finds it difficult to decide which one he likes best.

He wishes he could buy some of this lovely material as a present for his mother and sisters. That would be a nice surprise for them when he returned home to Dhamial.

25

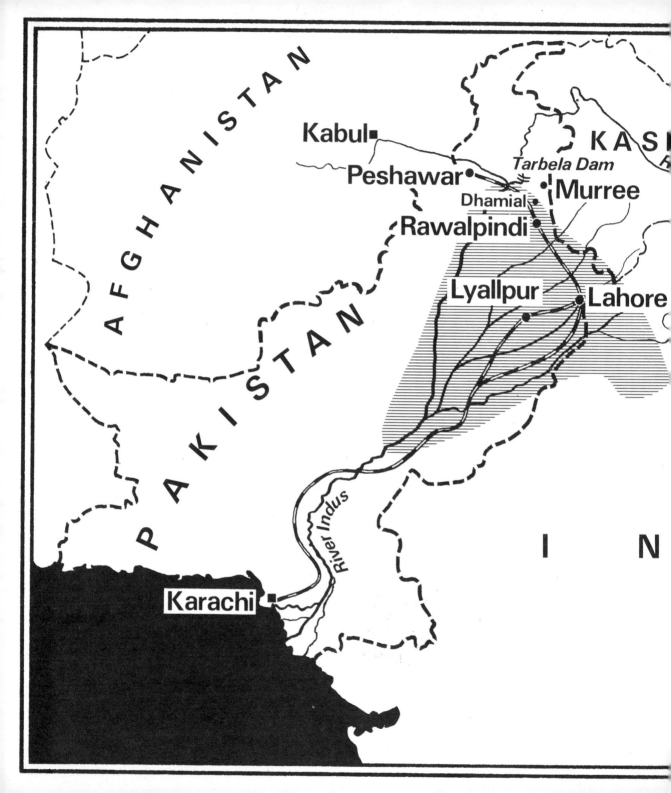